Maude and the Merry Christmas Tree

Written by Cynthia Fraser Graves
Illustrated by Nancy Bariluk-Smith

Cynthia Fraser Graves

[signature]

Maude and the Merry Christmas Tree

Written by Cynthia Fraser Graves
Illustrated by Nancy Bariluk-Smith

First Printing, 2020

ISBN 978-1-7329471-3-9
Androscoggin Press
PO Box 13
West Kennebunk, ME 04094

www.AndroscogginPress.com

Maude and the
Merry Christmas Tree

Dedicated to brave children everywhere.

Maude snuggled in bed.

When she remembered it was Saturday, and Christmas Tree Day, her eyes popped wide with excitement.

Maude and Mother would walk to Holyoke Avenue and into Christmas Tree Woods where hundreds of perfectly pointy Christmas trees grow.

Mother would bring shiny tinfoil to wrap and crinkle tight around a branch of the tree Maude picked to be their Christmas tree.

When Christmas got near, Daddy would go into the woods to find Maude's tree. He would cut it down and bring it home.

Maude imagined her tree would be taller than Daddy with fresh green needles, silvery tinsel, bright ornaments, and colored lights. Beneath the tree, mysterious presents would appear and a wonderful pine tree smell would spread through the house. Just thinking about Christmas made her happy, so happy that she laughed out loud and jumped out of bed.

Mother still left clothes out for Maude even though she was eight now. She put them on quickly, hoping she would surprise Mother and be ready.

Once downstairs, Maude looked for Mother everywhere. But Mother was not there.

She even went outdoors on the porch to look up and down the street. Maude saw that Mother's car was not in the driveway. Maude knew that Mother drove Daddy to work each day, but she was worried.

Mother was always here when she woke up.

"Maybe Mother forgot what day this is?" Maude wondered.

"Or, maybe I slept so late Mother went without me?" Maude thought.

Maude was hungry.

She went to the kitchen, made toast, buttered it, poured orange juice without spilling, and sat at the big table alone. As she chewed her toast, Maude thought about what to do.

By the time she finished her breakfast, she had an idea.

She would walk to the woods by herself to find her tree and surprise Mother. She knew the way and she knew where the tinfoil was kept. She went to the cupboard to get the tinfoil, feeling a little better now that she had a plan.

Maude was so anxious to get started that she didn't clean up after her breakfast.

She walked up Spruce Street, turned onto Holyoke Avenue and into Christmas Tree Woods.

As she walked, she pressed the tinfoil in her pocket and listened to it crinkle. She was imagining her Christmas tree. Even though she still wondered where Mother was, Maude was proud to be doing something so grown-up.

At last, giant green trees towered above her. She kept walking until they were all around. Maude felt warm from the walk. She unbuttoned her coat, took off her hat, and stuffed it into her pocket.

Now in the deep Maine woods, the trees got taller and taller. Maude didn't feel so brave here. Everything was so quiet. Somewhere she heard a bird chirp, reminding her she was not alone.

Maude wanted to find her Christmas tree right away. She would put the foil on the tree and go straight home in case Mother was looking for her. Maude zigzagged deeper into the woods.

Then she saw it! Her tree!! It had a pointy top and dark green branches with plenty of room to hang tinsel and ornaments. They would sing Christmas hymns around this tree. It was perfect.

Out came the tinfoil as Maude stood on tiptoes trying to reach the highest branch she could. She wrapped and crinkled the shiny tinfoil tight on the bough because it had to be there when Daddy came to find it. Maude backed up to see the foil shining on her tree.

That's when she saw that it had started to snow. At first, the lacy snowflakes delighted her. She ran around catching them on her tongue and trying to make snow angels, but there was not enough snow for that. When Maude got tired of playing, she sat under her tree to get out of the snow. Now, she really wanted to go home. It was getting late. She was worried about Mother.

She reached into her pocket for her hat but it wasn't there. Mother would not be happy about that.

Maude buttoned up her coat and looked up into the branches of her tree for the sparkle of tinfoil. But there was no tinfoil. This was not her tree. She peered as far out into the snowy woods as she could to find the sparkling branch of her tree, but it was nowhere to be seen.

"Oh no!" Maude thought.

Maude knew she had to find her way home.

She walked as quickly as she could looking for her tree but every tree was now coated in snow and looked the same. She walked and walked until the trees were so close together she couldn't fit between them anymore.

She was lost.

Maude sat under a roof of green branches. It was cold now and it was getting dark. She shivered and wrapped her arms around her knees. She had heard that a girl could get lost in the woods and never find her way home again. She began to cry. Her bursts of sobs sounded like bird chirps in the snow-quiet woods. She wanted her Mother.

"I have to be brave," she said. "I just have to."

Maude stood up and walked in the straightest line she could. As she walked, she heard "Cheep, cheep," above her. When she looked up, she saw that Redbird was watching her.

Maude called to the bird, hoping he would be her friend, and said, "Little bird, please show me the way home. I'm afraid and I'm lost. I want to see my Mother."

Redbird listened, cocking his head. The snow kept falling and the bird kept watching as Maude watched the bird. After a little while, Redbird hopped onto a high limb, swished his tail three times, and flew ahead of where Maude stood.

She hoped Redbird knew the way home and was helping her. She could not let herself think of Mother again for she would cry.

Redbird turned and flew back to perch on a branch just above Maude. He looked down at her, spread his bright red wings, jumped up and down and flew away once more. This time he flew three trees away from Maude and perched there, chirping for Maude to follow.

And she did.

Maude knew now that Redbird was showing her the way out of the forest so she could find her way home. She looked up to him and called out in the biggest voice she could, "I'm being brave Redbird. I will follow you."

Redbird flapped his wings, hopped a little dance and flew off again. This time, he perched five trees away from Maude, and once more, she followed, keeping her friend in sight through the falling snow. Tree to tree, the bird flew and Maude followed. The girl with no hat ran with her eyes pinned on Redbird, her bright red scout.

While Maude was running through the woods following Redbird, Mother arrived home. Her car ran out of gas when she took Daddy to work and it was a long while before she returned home. She worried about Maude all the way.

Once she saw the tinfoil container on the counter she knew where Maude had gone. She was in Christmas Tree Woods. Without even a pause to clean up Maude's breakfast dishes, Mother was on her way. She drove peering into the snow looking for her lost girl, praying she was safe.

Back in the woods, Redbird hip-hopped and flew ahead, tree by tree, with Maude following until she saw something shiny. It was the tinfoil on her Christmas tree. Beyond that, she could see the road. She was on her way. She began to run, Redbird still flying overhead.

When Maude finally stepped onto the road, she looked more like a snowman than a little girl. Redbird flew around and around, tweeting goodbye. He flashed his red feathers once more as he disappeared into Christmas Tree Woods. Maude called out a polite, "Thank you," and he vanished.

She felt better now; she knew her way home. But wait. The road, now under a thick cover of snow, stretched on both sides of her looking exactly the same. "Oh no," Maude whimpered, "I don't know where to go!" She looked one way, and then the other, trying to decide when she saw what looked like two bright eyes coming towards her.

But they weren't bright eyes, they were the headlights of a car, and the lights created a beautiful snow globe with Maude in the center. She was so delighted that she forgot how cold and afraid she was only moments ago.

Maude saw someone getting out of the car coming towards her. "Mother?" asked the little girl who looked like a snowman.

And Mother was there, kneeling to hold her close, almost crying for what might have happened to her girl. Mother spoke softly to her right there in the middle of the road, "Maudie, why did you come out here without me or Daddy?"

Maude tried to explain, but she was so cold and so tired and so happy that she just let Mother lift her and take her to the warmth and safety of the car.

A few weeks later, while they were decorating her Merry Christmas Tree, Maude told her family again the story of how her friend, Redbird, flew ahead of her and showed her the way out of the woods. Mother and Father smiled and winked at each other when they thought she wasn't watching.

She knew they didn't believe her but,
Maude knew what she knew.

She would never forget the kindness
of Redbird.

THE END

Meet the illustrator and writer:

Nancy Bariluk-Smith, Illustrator
Nancy's adventurous nature has taken her on backpacking journeys to Australia, New Zealand, and rural Alaska. Her lifelong passions revolve around color, nature, texture, and design. Nancy's latest endeavor is children's book illustration. She blends her unique images with the playful nature of childhood perspectives. In *Maude and the Merry Christmas Tree,* Nancy has hidden birds throughout the story for children to find. Nancy is a flourishing artist from Kennebunk, Maine. Learn more at NewBeginningsMaine.com.

Cynthia Fraser Graves, Writer
Cynthia is an accomplished writer, with published works including her latest novel, *Dusk On Route 1;* a memoir, *Never Count Crow: Love and Loss in Kennebunk, Maine;* an extensive poetry collection; and *A Year With Henry: A Twenty-first Century Blog.* In *Maude and the Merry Christmas Tree,* Cynthia reaches back to her childhood in Rumford, Maine—days absent of technology and the complications of the modern world. Learn more at CynthiaFraserGraves.com.

Be sure to watch for Maude's
next adventure:

Maude and the Holy Oak

Made in the USA
Monee, IL
01 October 2020